# AGREEMENT

I, _Henry Tubb_ , understand
[Print Name Here]

that in order for me to participate in

this book's activities, I must promise

to always do my homework.

No matter what.

_____
[Sign Here]

_____
[Date]

D1412461

ISBN 978-1-4521-4175-6

Manufactured by C & C Offset, Longgang, Shenzhen,
China, in April 2015.

Design by Ryan Hayes.
Typeset in 1820 Modern.

10 9 8 7 6 5 4 3 2 1

Chronicle Books LLC
680 Second Street, San Francisco, California 94107
Chronicle Books—we see things differently. Become part
of our community at www.chroniclekids.com.

# I DIDN'T DO MY HOMEWORK BECAUSE

## Doodle Book of Excuses

Davide Cali   Benjamin Chaud

chronicle books·san francisco

"So, why didn't you
do your homework?"

My teacher wanted an answer, but it's kind of a long story!
Maybe if you help me to tell it, she'll actually believe me.
I didn't do my homework because . . .

An airplane full of monkeys landed in our yard. They sure were an unruly bunch! How many monkeys do you see? Write your final tally here: _____

Monkey see! Spot and circle the monkey that is:
☐ Wearing a hat   ☐ Upside down   ☐ Holding the most pencils

Elves hid all of my pencils.

Before the elves showed up, I was coloring these dinosaurs for Science class. Since I can't find my pencils, will you help me to fill in the rest of the drawing?

I was abducted
by a UFO.

Not many kids get a chance to see what aliens really do in their spaceship, but I got to find out!

Draw an alien in the spaceship:

- Eating space-soup
- Playing a strange alien guitar
- Driving the spaceship
- Petting a dog . . . wait, IS that a dog?
- Dancing
- Doing homework (whoa, that looks hard!)

Giant lizards invaded my neighborhood. It was chaos! Help me sort out what happened. Find and circle:

☐ An upside-down car  ☐ Two people on scooters
☐ The lizard that ate my book

What if giant lizards came to *your* neighborhood?
Draw your house being attacked by the same lizards!

Now draw yourself! Are you looking out a window?
Hiding behind a tree? Outside fighting the lizards?

I was at my cat's funeral. If I had known you then, I would have invited you. Draw yourself at the funeral with me. Then, in the speech bubble, write the nice things you would have said about my cat.

My grandpa and his band were making too much noise, and I couldn't concentrate. How many instruments do you know in this picture? Write the names of each instrument next to the image.

☐ Trumpet ☐ Saxophone ☐ Banjo ☐ Piano ☐ Violin
☐ Acoustic guitar ☐ Electric guitar

Create your own band! Draw yourself playing the instrument you like best. Then draw some of your friends or family playing or singing with you! What would the name of your band be? Write it here:

A polar bear eating an ice cream cone

"But penguins live at the South Pole!"

We found a lost penguin, so we took him to the North Pole.
We encountered a lot of strange things in the snow and ice.
Retrace our steps and draw what we saw on our trek!

A majestic
ice palace

Santa Claus on
summer break

Snowmen sumo
wrestling

Yeti!

The neighbors asked if we could help them look for their armadillos.
Can you find and circle all five armadillos in this picture?

Wait a sec—my neighbors actually have SEVEN armadillos! Practice drawing a few using my handy armadillo drawing guide, then go back and add two more armadillos hiding somewhere in the scene.

## Armadillo Drawing Guide

Step 1: Round body

Step 2: Triangle face

Step 3: Two big ears, eyes, mouth, and nose

Step 4: Two little arms and two legs and feet

Step 5: Draw in the shell and the stomach and add lines to the ears.

You can practice your armadillos here:

Someone stole my pencils! I didn't get a good look at who it was, but maybe you did? Draw whoever (or whatever) stole them escaping out the window.

A famous director asked to use my bedroom to shoot his new movie.
Check out this crowd of people!

How many horses do you see? ____
How many cowboy hats? ____

Some strange birds made a nest on our roof. Uh-oh—I forgot to draw the birds! Can you draw some giant birds picking up my dog and me in their beaks?

Use this page to practice your bird drawing skills.
How many different kinds of birds can you draw?

My brother had his little problem again.

If you could turn into an animal every so often, what would you be?
Draw yourself with your "little problem" (like my brother)!

I had to help my sister retrieve her goldfish in its missing bowl. Can you find it?

My room is a mess. I couldn't find my homework anywhere!
Do you see it here?

How many different types of animals do you see?
Write the number here: ___

A tornado swept up all of my books. Actually, it swept up a lot more than that!
Draw what else got sucked up by the tornado.

So . . . why don't you believe me?

Oh no, I guess she's heard some of these excuses before. We'll just have to think up some more! On the next few pages, you'll get to create and illustrate your own set of excuses, but first, try out my Super Excuse Generator for more ideas!

# SUPER EXCUSE GENERATOR

Fill this out on your own, or, for *really* amazing excuses\*,
ask a friend to come up with the missing words. Don't
reveal the whole sentence until you've filled everything in,
and then see what wacky excuses you have created!

\*Warning: Excuses manufactured by the Super Excuse Generator may not be believed. Use with caution.

I didn't do my homework because

my _____ needed help
[family member]

_____ our _____
[verb ending in -ing]          [adjective]

_____.
[plural clothing item]

Now draw your excuse:

I didn't do my homework because

my friend, _____, and I
[your friend's name]

got trapped in a giant _____
[noun]

and had to battle a _____
[type of monster]

to escape.

Now draw your excuse:

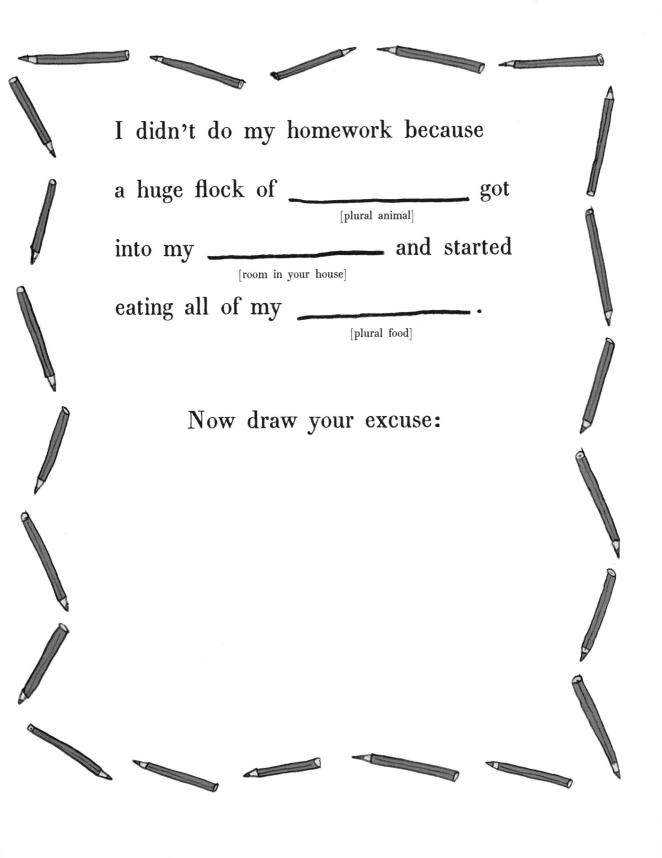

I didn't do my homework because

a huge flock of _____ got
[plural animal]

into my _____ and started
[room in your house]

eating all of my _____.
[plural food]


Now draw your excuse:

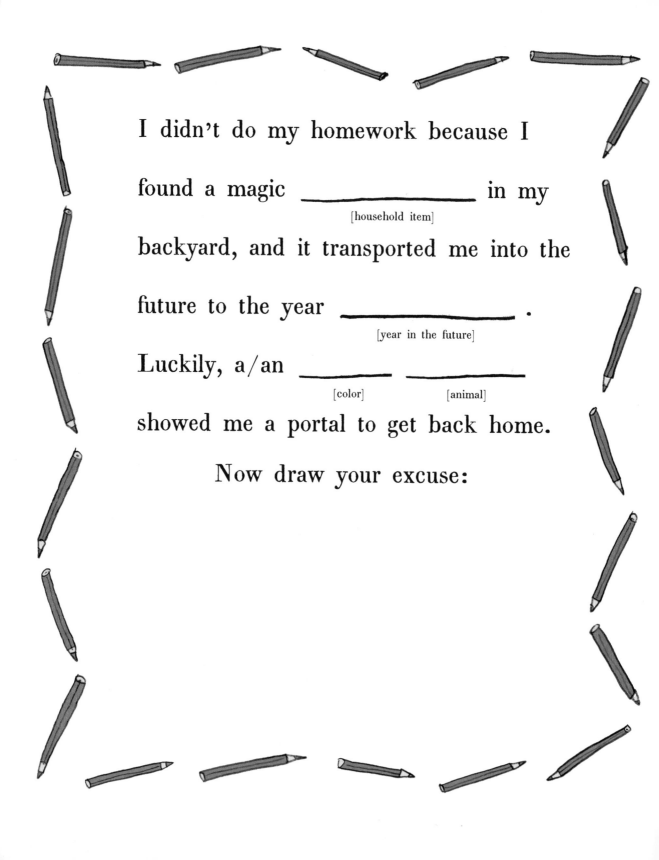

I didn't do my homework because I found a magic _____ in my
[household item]
backyard, and it transported me into the future to the year _____ .
[year in the future]
Luckily, a/an _____ _____
[color]       [animal]
showed me a portal to get back home.

Now draw your excuse:

I didn't do my homework because my

_____ needed a _____
[animal]                              [noun]

and then it _____.
[verb, past tense]

Now draw your excuse:

# YOUR COLORING ASSIGNMENT

My sister's rabbit chewed up all of my pencils and workbooks.
The rabbit also chewed through the walls! I always thought we
needed new wallpaper. Draw some new designs on all three walls.

YOUR COLORING ASSIGNMENT
Ahhh! Color in this lizard attack.

# YOUR COLORING ASSIGNMENT
These escaped convicts really didn't want me to do my homework.
Color in the scene.

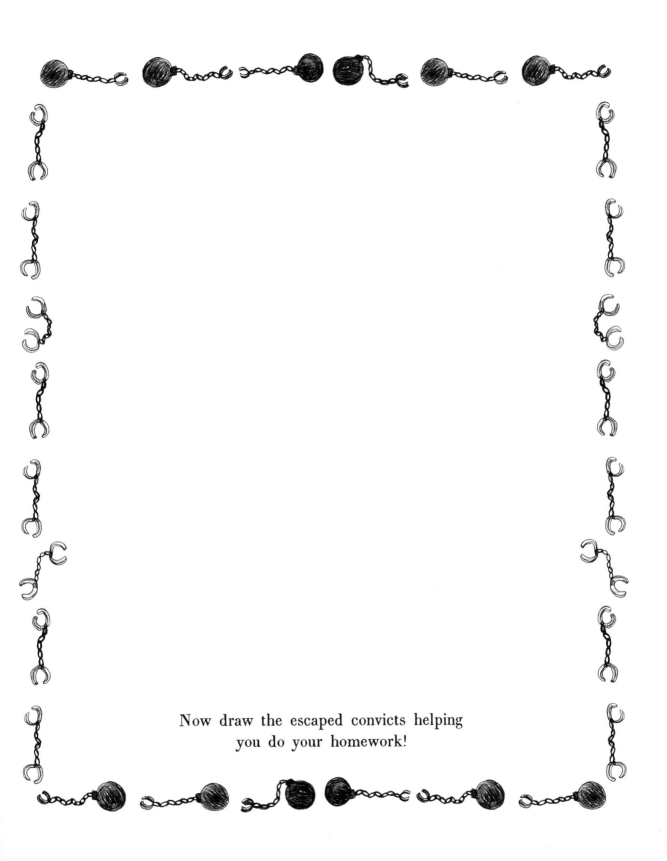

Now draw the escaped convicts helping
you do your homework!

# YOUR COLORING ASSIGNMENT

This rebellious robot really makes it tough to get homework done!
Color in the scene and you'll see what I mean . . .

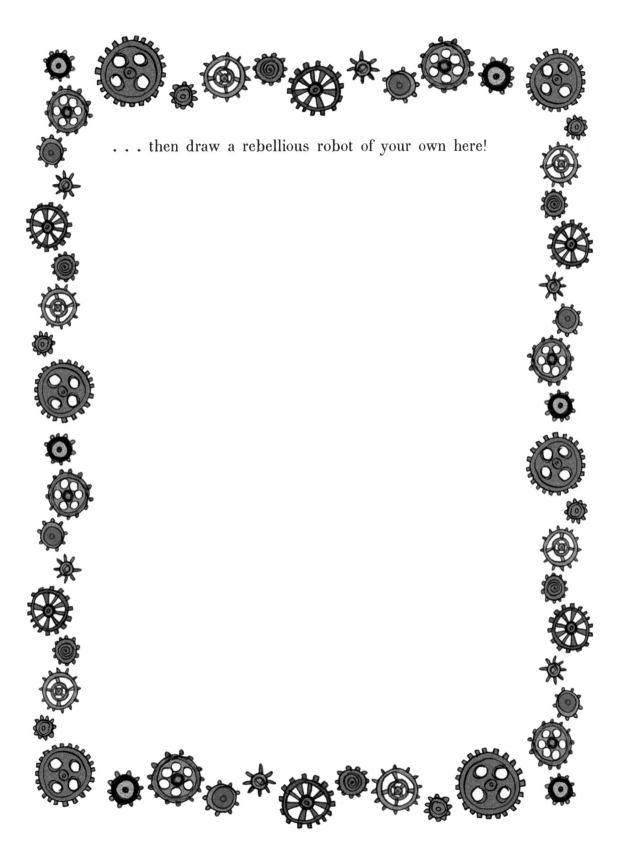

. . . then draw a rebellious robot of your own here!

# I DIDN'T DO MY HOMEWORK BECAUSE...
## THE COMIC

Draw what is happening in each frame!

An airplane full of monkeys landed in our yard.

Then the monkeys ran everywhere, and it took a while to catch them all.

# I DIDN'T DO MY HOMEWORK BECAUSE...
## THE COMIC

Draw what is happening in each frame!

I was abducted by a UFO.

Some aliens were very interested in my workbooks.

And they were curious about
my pencils, too.

Then they asked me to explain
some math problems.

I tried to help them out,
but I couldn't.

So they set me free. But they
kept my workbooks.

# I DIDN'T DO MY HOMEWORK BECAUSE...
## THE COMIC

Draw what is happening in each frame!

Just when I started to do my homework . . .

. . . we were attacked by Vikings.

Vikings?! How am I supposed to believe that?

Well, they weren't *real* Vikings.

But it was just some people playing a game.

At some point, the gamers started arguing.

So they asked me to settle their argument.

But the loser was not happy. And that's why we were attacked.

# I DIDN'T DO MY HOMEWORK BECAUSE...
## THE COMIC

Draw what is happening
in each frame!

Giant rats invaded my
neighborhood.

Oh, my goodness! What did you do?

Well, first we tried to get rid of the rats with giant lizards.

|  |  |
|---|---|
| But then we had giant lizards everywhere. | So then we thought: "Giant eagles!" |
| But then we had giant eagles everywhere. | So we just moved to another neighborhood. |

# I DIDN'T DO MY HOMEWORK BECAUSE...
## THE COMIC

Draw what is happening in each frame!

We found a sleeping penguin, so we thought he was probably lost and we took him to the North Pole.

It was so cold, we had to wear giant snowsuits.

But then we realized that penguins live in the South Pole.

So we took him there instead.

Once at the South Pole, we realized that he wasn't a penguin at all.

So I didn't do my homework because of a guy named Brian in a penguin suit.

# I DIDN'T DO MY HOMEWORK BECAUSE...
## THE COMIC

Draw what is happening
in each frame!

We ran out of firewood,
so I sacrificed my books to
stay warm.

My textbooks went first . . .

Then my math workbooks.

And some pencils, too.

And did you also sacrifice your comics collection?

Oh, no! At that point, we already had a huge fire!

Now it's time for you to draw your own *I Didn't Do My Homework Because* . . . comic strip! Just fill in the first comic panel with your excuse, and then write three more sentences explaining what happens next. Then draw in each comic frame to complete your strip!

Now it's time for you to draw your own *I Didn't Do My Homework Because* . . . comic strip! Just fill in the first comic panel with your excuse, and then write three more sentences explaining what happens next. Then draw in each comic frame to complete your strip!

Now it's time for you to draw your own *I Didn't Do My Homework Because* . . . comic strip! Just fill in the first comic panel with your excuse, and then write three more sentences explaining what happens next. Then draw in each comic frame to complete your strip!

Now it's time for you to draw your own *I Didn't Do My Homework Because* . . . comic strip! Just fill in the first comic panel with your excuse, and then write three more sentences explaining what happens next. Then draw in each comic frame to complete your strip!

Now it's time for you to draw your own *I Didn't Do My Homework Because . . .* comic strip! Just fill in the first comic panel with your excuse, and then write three more sentences explaining what happens next. Then draw in each comic frame to complete your strip!

I've already used these excuses, so I'll let you borrow them, free of charge. Draw your own version of the excuses on each page!

I didn't do my homework because . . .

I had to help my grandpa paint some flowers on his van.

I didn't do my homework because . . .

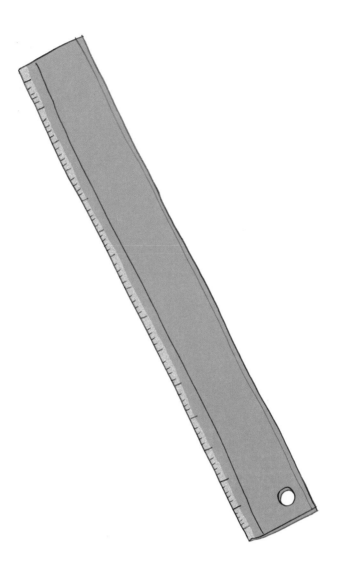

My ruler grew legs and ran right off my desk.

I didn't do my homework because . . .

I had a pillow fight with my brother, and it got a little out of hand.
Draw what happened . . .

Remember my brother?!

I didn't do my homework because . . .

The elves got me, once again.

I didn't do my homework because . . .

Little rabbit, big city! My sister's pet rabbit got
lost in a bustling city, and I had to help her find it.
Draw the skyscrapers we saw on our search.

Then draw the rest of the city here.

I didn't do my homework because . . .

I lost my dog in a pumpkin field. Draw all of the huge pumpkins. (And the small ones, too.)

I didn't do my homework because . . .

A superhero let me borrow his suit and superpowers for the day.
Draw my awesome incognito adventures.

I didn't do my homework because . . .

My room suddenly had zero gravity.
Draw the effect it had on me and my homework.

I didn't do my homework because . . .

INO SCENE - DO NOT CROSS - DINO SCENE - DO NOT CROSS

My brother and I found a dinosaur skeleton in our
yard, and we had to get it ready for a museum.
Draw the skeleton!

DINO SCENE - DO NOT CROSS- DINO SCENE - DO NOT C

I didn't do my homework because . . .

We had a problem with zombies. Draw them.

I didn't do my homework because . . .

Some animals escaped from the zoo and wandered into our backyard,
and it took hours to move them away. Draw the animals.

I didn't do my homework because . . .

I had to help my uncle create a
clone of me so the clone could
do my homework.

But when the clone came to life, he didn't want
to do any homework . . .

. . . so we tried to convince him.

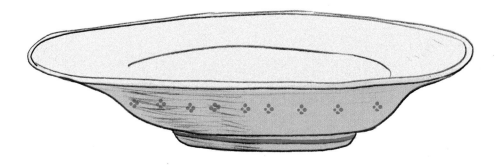

Draw the special treat I brought the clone to
reward him for his homework skills.

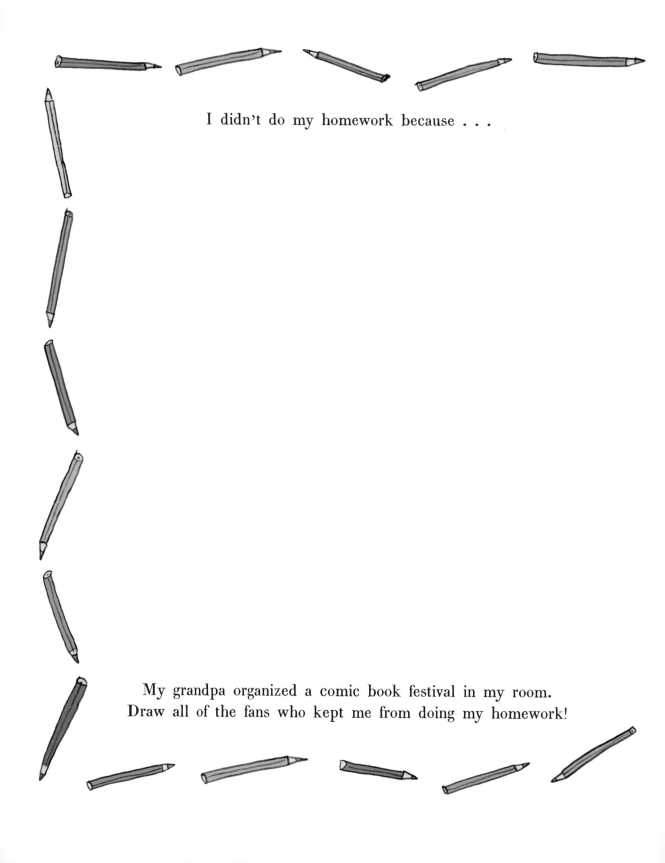

I didn't do my homework because . . .

My grandpa organized a comic book festival in my room.
Draw all of the fans who kept me from doing my homework!

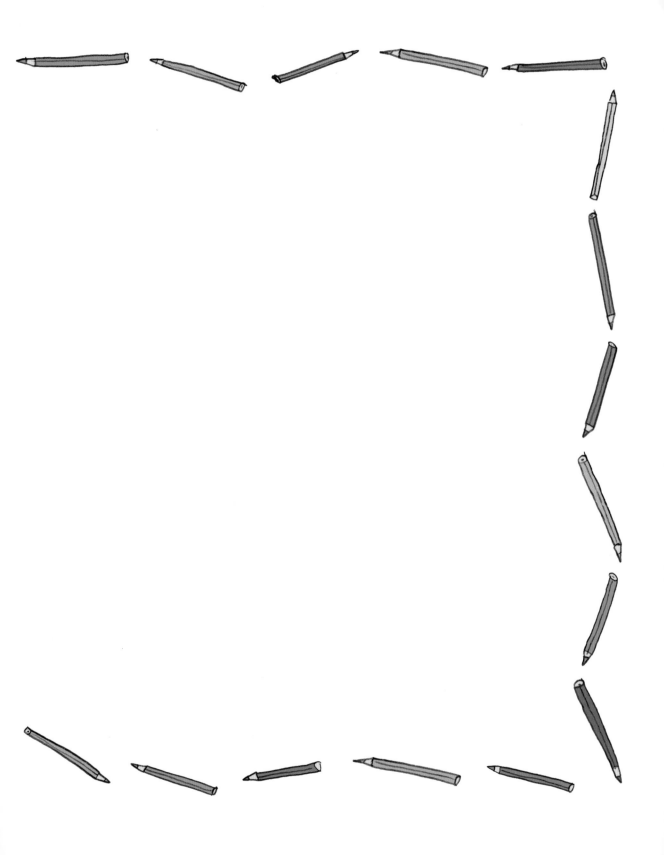

I didn't do my homework because . . .

We had a gigantic snowball fight against the neighbors.

Really? A snowball
fight . . . in the *spring*?
How is that possible?

Well, my uncle had kept
snow in the freezer since
the winter.

I didn't do my homework because . . .

—

I was stuck in a labyrinth all afternoon.
Draw a maze around me.

I didn't do my homework because . . .

My sister needed to use my room for her dance recital.
Draw the big performance and all of the costumes.

I didn't do my homework because . . .

My grandpa wanted me to teach him how to skateboard.
How could I say no?!

I didn't do my homework because . . .

I had to help my uncle conduct an important scientific experiment.

But what about your
*science homework*?!

I think you're ready! Now it's time to come up with your *own* excuses. Write one at the bottom of the page, and then draw your excuse!

I didn't do my homework because . . .

I didn't do my homework because . . .

I didn't do my homework because . . .

_____

I didn't do my homework because . . .

_____

I didn't do my homework because . . .

_____

I didn't do my homework because . . .

I didn't do my homework because . . .

_____

I didn't do my homework because . . .

_____

I didn't do my homework because . . .

_____

I didn't do my homework because . . .

_____

I didn't do my homework because . . .

_____

I didn't do my homework because . . .

I didn't do my homework because . . .

_____

I didn't do my homework because . . .

_____

I didn't do my homework because . . .

_____

I didn't do my homework because . . .

_____

I didn't do my homework because . . .

I didn't do my homework because . . .

_____

I didn't do my homework because . . .

I didn't do my homework because . . .

_____

I didn't do my homework because . . .

_____

I didn't do my homework because . . .

I didn't do my homework because . . .

I didn't do my homework because . . .

I didn't do my homework because . . .

_____

I didn't do my homework because . . .

_____

I didn't do my homework because . . .

_____

I didn't do my homework because . . .

I didn't do my homework because . . .

_____

I didn't do my homework because . . .

_____

I didn't do my homework because . . .

_____

I didn't do my homework because . . .

# I DIDN'T DO MY HOMEWORK BECAUSE...

Davide Cali  Benjamin Chaud

chronicle books · san francisco

# I DIDN'T DO MY HOMEWORK BECAUSE...

Davide Cali  Benjamin Chaud

chronicle books · san francisco

I had to attend a book signing to autograph copies of my first book,
*I Didn't Do My Homework Because* . . . Since you helped out with
this doodle book, I want you to sign these copies, too!

Whew. That was a lot
of excuses.

Alright. Now, time
to do my homework.
Really. I mean it . . .